A Turtle Ranch Adventure

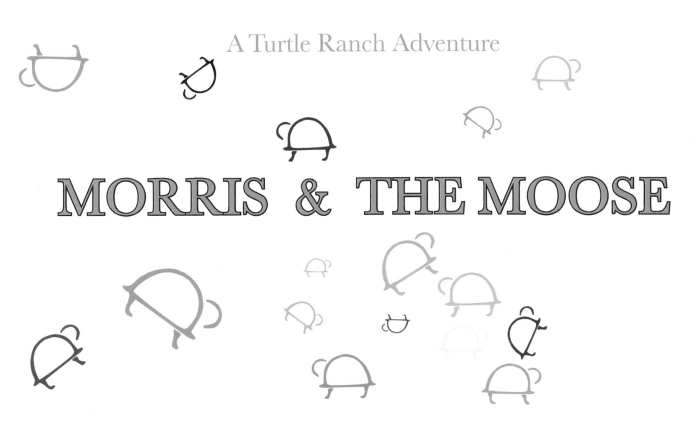

MORRIS & THE MOOSE

written by Kate Wiltshire & illustrated by Kathleen Watson

for Dan Dowling

Designed by Turtle Books

This book belongs to:

My favorite dog is:

this a true story...

Meet Benny the Turtle - He is hiding 20 times throughout this book . See if you can find him.

It was a blistering hot summer day at Turtle Ranch.

Tom the big white dog was standing in
the water trough trying to cool down.
Kate was washing a yellow horse.

Charlie Francis was lying in the shade
under a wagon watching Alice chase a
cat.

Jack was sniffing a horse poo while Rosie
dug a small hole.

Morris was helping Rancher Robin train the
Clydesdale Horses in the arena.

6

Kate fed her big yellow horse some hay and said to the dogs, "it's too hot to work today, lets go for a swim."

The happy dogs ran to Kate wagging their tails,
they bounced around in excitement.

 The dogs jumped into the big red truck
and they drove through a field of tall
green grass.

Kate parked close to the river and all the dogs
jumped out of the truck eager to go for a swim.

The dogs had to bounce high when they ran
so they could see where they were going!

How many dogs can you count?

Suddenly everyone stood very still. Something
was wrong. "Shhhh" said Kate

Rumble, Rumble, Thump, Crash. Something
was coming. What do you think it could be?

It was a big brown Moose...
He was very grumpy.

Kate and the dogs started running back to the truck as fast as they could go. The giant moose charged behind them.

The dogs jumped into the truck with Kate.
One, two, three, four, five and...

"Oh no!" Where was Morris?

Brave Morris was growling at the Moose "Grrrrrrrr Grrrrr." The surprised Moose stamped his giant hoof hard onto the ground.

Morris ran as fast as he could go with the mad
Moose at his heels.

 Morris and the Moose plunged into the cold
river and made a giant splash. Morris barked
loudly at the Moose. "WOOF WOOF"

The Moose swam across the river and galloped away.

Meanwhile, Kate and the dogs sat in the red truck. It was hot and squashy.

They waited for Morris to come back. They waited and waited. Kate was getting worried.

"Morris where are you" Kate called again and again. "Morris!"

Suddenly the grass began to move and rustle,
everyone looked up. Guess What? It was
Morris. The Moose was gone.

26

Kate opened the door and everyone piled
out of the truck.

PHEW it was hot!

Morris had water dripping from his fur. He wagged his tail and shook water from his back soaking his friends from head to tail.

"Thank you Morris" exclaimed a relieved Kate
"You saved us".

"Lets go swimming" laughed Kate.

Everyone jumped into the river splashing
water everywhere.

THE END....

MORRIS

Morris has appeared in films and commercials his whole life.

He is a 10 year old Australian Cattle Dog and was born on Turtle Ranch.

TOM

Tom is a rescue dog who appeared in the Budweiser Super Bowl commercial "Spot"

He is 9 years old and keeps us forever entertained at Turtle Ranch.

CHARLIE FRANCIS

Charlie Francis trained alongside the
Budweiser Clydesdales for the
Super Bowl Commercial "Puppy Love".
She is 3 years old. She loves playing with
her doggie and human friends
 at Turtle Ranch.

ALICE

Alice The Wonder Dog is 4 years old.

She can run very fast and loves to be pampered. She is always happy and full of fun.

JACK

Jack was born in Dubois Wyoming and is 8 years old.

He appeared in the extreme bike movie UnReal as an extra and has done plenty of modeling for catalogues.

ROSIE RED CHEEKS

Rosie Red Cheeks was born at Turtle Ranch and is 9 years old.

She loves to hang out at the homestead and guard the house while we go to work.

ABOUT THE CONTRIBUTORS

Kate Wiltshire & Kathleen Watson met 20 years ago
in Wyoming and have been friends ever since.

Kate lives & works at Turtle Ranch in Wyoming.
Her dogs and life on the ranch are her inspiration. turtleranch.net

Kathleen works from her studios in Australia & America
kathleenisomwatson.com

This is their first collaboration.

Find us on Facebook - https://www.facebook.com/turtleranchbooks/ &
https://www.facebook.com/Morris-Wiltshire-182869291805757/

Special thanks to Shell, Tiffany, Kristy & Liv for your editing and support.

CPSIA information can be obtained at www.ICGtesting.com
Printed in the USA
BVIW12n0744201216
471228BV00010B/11